A NOTE TO PARENTS

When your children are ready to "step into reading," giving them the right books—and lots of them—is as crucial as giving them the right food to eat. **Step into Reading Books** present exciting stories and information reinforced with lively, colorful illustrations that make learning to read fun, satisfying, and worthwhile. They are priced so that acquiring an entire library of them is affordable. And they are beginning readers with an important difference—they're written on four levels.

Step 1 Books, with their very large type and extremely simple vocabulary, have been created for the very youngest readers. **Step 2 Books** are both longer and slightly more difficult. **Step 3 Books,** written to mid-second-grade reading levels, are for the child who has acquired even greater reading skills. **Step 4 Books** offer exciting nonfiction for the increasingly proficient reader.

Children develop at different ages. **Step into Reading Books,** with their four levels of reading, are designed to help children become good—and interested—readers *faster.* The grade levels assigned to the four steps—preschool through grade 1 for Step 1, grades 1 through 3 for Step 2, grades 2 and 3 for Step 3, and grades 2 through 4 for Step 4—are intended only as guides. Some children move through all four steps very rapidly; others climb the steps over a period of several years. These books will help your child "step into reading" in style!

For Blanche Etra,
a peerless friend
—S. S.

Photo credits: Annie Oakley Foundation Collection, p. 40; The Bettmann Archive, p. 4; Courtesy Buffalo Bill Historical Center, Cody, Wyoming, p. 28; Courtesy of The Cincinnati Historical Society, p. 16; Circus World Museum, Baraboo, Wisconsin, p. 35; Garst Museum, Greenville, Ohio, p. 48; National Anthropological Archives, Smithsonian Institution, p. 26, Western History Collections, University of Oklahoma Library, p. 38.

Library of Congress Cataloging-in-Publication Data
Spinner, Stephanie.
  Little Sure Shot : the story of Annie Oakley / by Stephanie Spinner ; illustrated by José Miralles.
    p. cm. – (Step into reading. Step 3 book)
  Summary: A biography of the poor young farmgirl who went on to become a famous sharpshooter with Buffalo Bill's Wild West Show.
  ISBN 0-679-83432-X (pbk.) – ISBN 0-679-93432-4 (lib. bdg.)
  1. Oakley, Annie, 1860–1926–Juvenile literature. 2. Shooters of firearms–United States–Biography–Juvenile literature. 3. Entertainers–United States–Biography–Juvenile literature. 4. Wild west shows–Juvenile literature. [1. Oakley, Annie, 1860–1926. 2. Sharpshooters. 3. Entertainers.] I. Miralles, José, ill. II. Title. III. Series.
GV1157.03S68 1993
799.3′092–dc20   92-17014
[B]

Manufactured in the United States of America 10 9 8 7 6 5 4 3 2 1

STEP INTO READING is a trademark of Random House, Inc.

Step into Reading

LITTLE
SURE SHOT
THE STORY OF ANNIE OAKLEY

By Stephanie Spinner
Illustrated by José Miralles

A Step 3 Book

Random House 🏠 New York

1

Little Sure Shot

It is the fall of 1869. A nine-year-old girl sits alone in a run-down farmhouse. She is worried. Her family is very poor. They work hard, but they have no money. They never have enough to eat. The girl wants to help.

She has an idea. That is why she is in the house all by herself. The idea scares her a little.

The girl looks at her father's gun. No one in the family is allowed to shoot it. Her mother says it is only for protection. But the girl knows that guns are good for hunting. She has watched men shoot birds and animals for food. Now she wants to try.

The girl takes the gun off the wall. It is heavy. It is taller than she is. It smells of oil and gunpowder.

Mama will not like this, thinks the girl. But I'm going to do it anyhow. I have to.

The girl takes the gun into the woods. She walks quietly. When she sees a squirrel, she freezes. Squirrel stew! she thinks.

She lifts the heavy gun to her shoulder. She looks down the barrel and aims. Then she pulls the trigger.

Crack! When the gun fires, it whacks her in the face. She falls down hard. Annie, she thinks, you are a fool!

But when she gets up, she sees that she has hit her target. She is not a fool. Not at all.

Her family will have a good meal that night. She has found a way to feed them.

And though she does not know it, shooting will make her famous. The girl's name is Phoebe Ann Moses. But the world will know her as Annie Oakley.

2

Could one day change everything? Yes!
Life was never the same for the Moses
family after Annie picked up that gun.

She put food on the table. She even
sold the game she shot. A fancy restaurant
bought the quail and grouse. A trader
named Frenchy La Motte bought the
foxes, minks, and raccoons for their

skins. For the first time ever, Annie's family didn't have to worry about money.

But Annie couldn't forget the hard times. Her father had died when she was only five. Her mother married again, but she still struggled to work as a country nurse and take care of her children. They wore old, raggedy clothes. Often they

went hungry. There was never any money
for books. That meant Annie and her
brothers and sisters couldn't go to school.

Annie wished she could read and
write. Once she even took a job so she
could go to school. But the other children
made fun of her hand-me-down dresses
and her worn-out shoes. They even made

fun of her name, calling her Moses-Poses. Annie never went back.

That bothered Annie's mother. She wanted her daughter to get an education. And even though she was proud of Annie's skill, she didn't really like her using a gun. Guns were for boys. In the 1870s girls were supposed to be dainty and delicate—little ladies.

Annie wanted to be a lady. But shooting was important to her. Why couldn't a lady be strong, and brave, and a crack shot, too? Annie just couldn't understand.

Then, when she was fifteen, a letter came from her married sister, Lyda. "Send Annie to live with me and Joe," she wrote. "Cincinnati is a wonderful city. Annie will like it. She can go to a good school here. She can become a young lady."

That was all Annie's mother had
to read. The next thing Annie knew,
her bags were packed and she was on
her way.

3

Lyda was right—Annie did like Cincinnati.
She liked the crowds, the bright lights,
and the steamboats on the Ohio River.
But best of all, she liked the shooting
galleries. There she could shoot to her
heart's content. The tin ducks gliding by
were so much easier to hit than live birds!

One day Annie noticed a man watching
her shoot. When she put down her gun,
he came over and tipped his hat.

"Miss, would you like to earn some
money doing that?" he asked.

"How?" said Annie.

"In a shooting match," he said.
"Winner gets a hundred dollars."

Annie was amazed. A hundred dollars
was a lot of money—more than many
people earned in a year.

"I'll do it," said Annie.

But on the day of the match Annie got nervous. A crowd had gathered to watch. And she was up against a famous sharpshooter named Frank Butler. He went around the country giving shooting exhibitions to crowds even bigger than this one.

When Frank Butler saw Annie, he laughed. "That little thing?" he said. "She's only a girl!"

Annie's cheeks burned. Suddenly she didn't care that Frank Butler was famous. Or that he was wearing medals from all the contests he'd won. She forgot about being nervous. I'm going to win this, she decided.

Butler fired the first shot. It was a hit. Then Annie fired. Her shot was a hit, too.

Target after target was thrown into

the air. Time after time, both Annie and
Frank hit them. Then, on his last turn,
Frank Butler missed. The crowd got
very quiet.

This was Annie's chance. She raised
her gun. She took aim, fired—and hit
the target. She had won!

The crowd cheered. They had never
seen anything like Annie. Neither had

Frank Butler. "That little girl is one heck
of a shot!" he said. "One *heck* of a shot!"

After the match Frank could not stop
thinking about her. She was not only a
heck of a shot, she was also very pretty.

Frank called on Annie at Lyda's
house. They began to see a lot of each
other. A year later they were married.

4

Annie was happy with Frank. He was a good husband. He was handsome and kind. And it was fun being married to a famous sharpshooter.

Annie loved to watch his act. Frank could hit three glass balls that were thrown into the air at the same time. He could shoot the number off a playing card. He could even shoot an apple into pieces— off the head of his dog!

Soon after they were married, Frank took his act on tour. Annie stayed at the farm with her mother. There she finally learned to read and write, so she could write letters to Frank.

There was something else Annie wanted to learn—trick shooting. She wanted to surprise Frank when he came back. So every day she went out into the

fields to practice. And by the time Frank
returned, Annie could do all the stunts
he did.

It was a good thing, too. One day
Frank's partner got sick and couldn't
perform. There was no one to take his
place—except Annie.

Annie was not used to stages, or
bright lights, or large audiences. She
missed her first shot, and the audience

groaned. There were boos and hisses.

"Go, home, girlie!" someone shouted.
Annie's eyes flashed. She took a deep
breath and shot again. This time she
scored a hit. Each shot after that was
perfect. Soon the audience was clapping
and cheering. The little girl with the big
gun had won them over.

And Frank Butler had a new partner
for his sharpshooting act!

Now that Annie and Frank were partners on stage, Annie wanted a special stage name. She remembered the shooting match where she and Frank first met. It was held at a place called Oakley. That's it, she thought. And from that time on, her name was Annie Oakley.

The sharpshooting act of Butler and Oakley traveled all through the Midwest. Annie loved going from town to town with Frank. And her shooting kept getting better. Soon she was doing things no one else could do—not even her husband.

She could shoot a dime out of his hand. She could shoot the end off a lit cigarette that he held in his mouth. She could shoot bending over backward. She could even shoot behind her by looking in a mirror—or a knife blade!

It was no wonder that her fame grew. One night a great Sioux chief called

Sitting Bull came to the show. As Annie
hit target after target with perfect aim,
Sitting Bull jumped to his feet. *"Watanya
cicilia!"* he cried in Sioux. "Little Sure
Shot!"

Sitting Bull and Annie became good friends. The great chief even adopted her. He made her a Sioux princess. He gave her many gifts—a quiver of his best arrows and a beautiful feather headdress. But Annie's favorite gift from Sitting Bull was the name he gave her—Little Sure Shot.

5

Soon the whole world would know of Little Sure Shot—all because of a man named Buffalo Bill.

Once a pony express rider, then a hunter, Buffalo Bill knew that Americans loved the West. So he put together a traveling show—part circus, part rodeo—with all the things that made the West

exciting. His show had cowboys. It had
Indians. It had wild horses, buffalo,
music, parades, horse races, and a
stagecoach. It had everything but a star.
  Annie changed that.

Her act in Buffalo Bill's show went something like this:

"Ladies and gentlemen!" cries the announcer. "The Wild West presents the lovely lass of the Western Plains, Little Sure Shot—the one and only Annie Oakley!"

Annie comes riding in on a fast little pinto pony. She wears a buckskin dress with fringe and a big hat pinned with a silver star. Her long brown hair flies out behind her. She smiles at the audience.

A cowboy rides into the ring. He races past Annie hurling clay targets into the air. Annie leans way down from her galloping pony. A pistol is on the ground. Now it's in her hand!

Bang! Bang! Bang! She hits each target at a full gallop. Then she leaps off her pony. She runs over to a table and picks up a rifle. Her husband, Frank, throws six glass balls into the air. Just for an instant they are points of light. Then Annie aims —and they're gone.

Frank whirls a glass ball on a string. Annie watches it in a mirror. She aims her gun backward. *Bang!* The ball disappears.

Now Frank holds up a playing card—
the ace of hearts. Annie stands thirty feet
away. She takes aim. *Bang!* Her bullet
goes right through the heart at the center
of the card.

But Annie's not finished yet. Frank turns the card sideways. Is it possible? Can she do it?

Yes! She shoots the card in half. Thousands of fans leap to their feet, shouting Annie's name. She smiles and curtsies. Then she's on her pony again, racing out of the ring.

She takes the hearts of the audience with her. And makes Buffalo Bill's Wild West show the most popular entertainment in America.

6

In 1887 Annie found herself on a ship
crossing the vast Atlantic Ocean. She and
Frank, and the entire Wild West show—
performers, animals, even a stagecoach
and two covered wagons—were going to
England.

It was the year of Queen Victoria's
golden jubilee. She had ruled England for
fifty years—longer than any other monarch

in its history. The whole country was celebrating. Visitors, including many royal visitors, were coming to England from all over the world. The Wild West show was invited to come, too.

Annie and Frank enjoyed being on the ocean. But other passengers felt differently. The cowboys were seasick. And the Indians were afraid. An old Indian prophecy warned against traveling across water. During the first week at sea, a terrible storm hit. All ninety-seven Indians on board sang their death songs for two days.

Finally the voyage ended. The show set up its tents and tepees on a huge field in London. Annie got ready to perform in front of forty thousand people.

It was the biggest crowd she had ever seen. But if Annie was nervous, no one

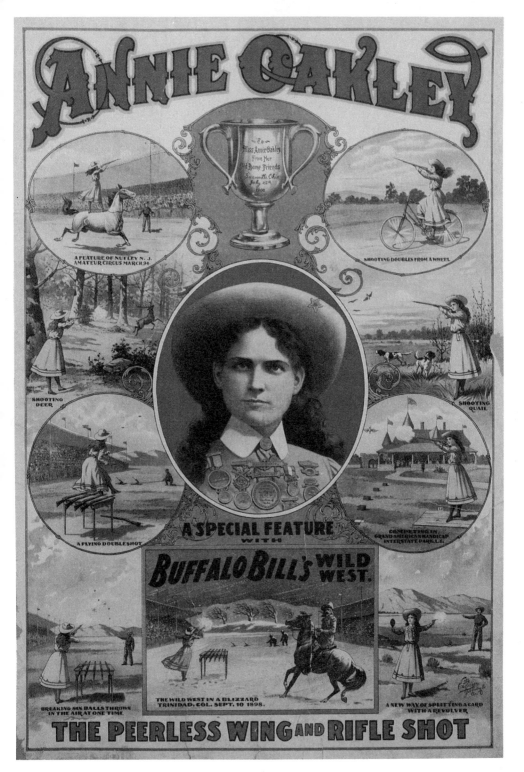

could tell. Her shooting was perfect.
The audience went wild. The next day
newspapers called her Annie Oakley of
the Magic Gun. After that, everyone in
London wanted tickets.

Then a message came from
Buckingham Palace. Queen Victoria

herself was coming to the show—but only
for an hour. Everyone was very excited.
The queen almost never went out in
public.

Annie came on at the end of the show.
She could see Queen Victoria far across
the ring—a little old lady in black sitting

on a platform covered with flowers. The show was running late. The queen's hour was almost up.

Annie was disappointed. Guess she won't see much of me, she thought. But the queen did not leave. She sat through Annie's entire act. And when it was finished, she asked to meet her!

The queen was tiny and frail. But her eyes sparkled as she pinned a medal to Annie's buckskin dress. "You are a very, *very* clever little girl," she said.

7

The queen was the first royal person
Annie met. But she was not the last. Soon
Annie found herself pointing a gun at a
prince!

The emperor of Germany and his son,
Crown Prince Wilhelm, had seen Annie in
London. They wanted to see her again.
They sent her an invitation. Would the

young American lady shoot for them in
Germany?

She would.

As usual, Annie put on a great show.
She shot clay pigeons. She shot live
pigeons. She shot glass balls. Her
audience began to applaud her. They
were German princes, generals, and
military men—all good shots. They had

heard about Annie. But they had not believed this tiny American woman could shoot so well.

She had surprised them. Now their stern faces were smiling.

Things were going smoothly. Annie was pleased. Then she got the surprise of her life.

Crown Prince Wilhelm stepped into the ring. He lit a cigarette and put it in his mouth. An aide came up to Annie.

"The prince commands you to put his cigarette out by shooting off the tip," he said. "He says he has seen you do this and now you must do it again."

Annie's heart began to thud. She had done this trick many times before—with her husband, Frank. But Crown Prince Wilhelm was the future emperor of Germany! What if she missed? What if

she hit the prince? That was too terrible
to think about.

Annie gathered up all her courage.
She walked thirty paces from the prince.

She raised her rifle and smoothly took aim. *Crack!* The prince's head jerked back. His cigarette was only a stub. Annie had made the shot.

The audience broke into wild cheers. Crown Prince Wilhelm gave Annie a bow. She smiled sweetly. Then she left the ring. Frank was waiting for her.

"That was really something, Annie," he said.

"That was the scariest moment of my life," she answered.

8

After three winters in Europe, Annie really missed America. She and Frank sailed home and built a house in New Jersey. They settled down—for a while.

It wasn't long before Buffalo Bill was in touch, though. The Wild West show was booked to play in Chicago, and then in New York. Would Annie star again?

She was happy to. In fact, Annie
stayed with the show for almost seventeen
years—longer than any other performer.
Then, one night in 1901, the show was in
a terrible train wreck. Annie was hurt
badly. The shock was so great that her
long dark hair turned completely white.

It was time, she decided, for a change.
She and Frank left the show for good.

But that wasn't the end of Annie's
career. Once she was well again, she was
back on stage. She starred in a show

called *The Western Girl,* which was written just for her. She competed in shooting matches, won a fortune in prize money, and gave a lot of it to charities that helped poor children. She taught thousands of women how to shoot. She performed for the troops during World War I. She raised money for the Red Cross. And when the war was over, she kept on shooting. She celebrated her sixty-second birthday by hitting a hundred clay pigeons in a row!

Annie Oakley died in November 1926.

Frank died three weeks later. They are buried side by side in Ohio.

Annie first picked up a gun more than a hundred years ago. Life was very different for women then. They stayed at home and took care of the children. They did not shoot guns. They did not compete against men. They did not move freely in the world, winning fame and fortune.

Annie Oakley did all of these things. She was one in a million.